Amelia Jane
Stories

More Amelia Jane published by Egmont

Naughty Amelia Jane
Amelia Jane is Naughty Again!
Good Idea, Amelia Jane
Amelia Jane Again

Enid Blyton

Amelia Jane
Stories

EGMONT

EGMONT

We bring stories to life

First published in Great Britain 1954 by Newnes
as part of *More About Amelia Jane!*
This edition published 2013 by Egmont UK Limited
The Yellow Building, 1 Nicholas Road London, W11 4AN

ISBN 978 0 6035 6946 3

1 3 5 7 9 10 8 6 4 2

www.egmont.co.uk

A CIP catalogue record for this title is available from the British Library

Printed and bound in China

56126/1

Stay safe online. Any website addresses listed in this book are correct at the time of going to print.
However, Egmont is not responsible for content hosted by third parties. Please be aware that
online content can be subject to change and websites can contain content that is unsuitable for
children. We advise that all children are supervised when using the internet.

EGMONT LUCKY COIN

Our story began over a century ago, when seventeen-year-old
Egmont Harald Petersen found a coin in the street.

He was on his way to buy a flyswatter, a small hand-operated
printing machine that he then set up in his tiny apartment.

The coin brought him such good luck that today Egmont has
offices in over 30 countries around the world. And that lucky
coin is still kept at the company's head offices in Denmark.

Contents

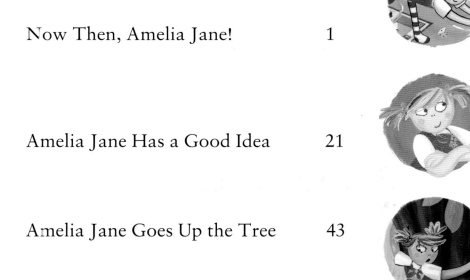

Now Then, Amelia Jane!

Now Then, Amelia Jane!

Amelia Jane, the big naughty doll in the nursery, was doing a bit of sewing. She sat in the corner, her head bent over her work, sewing away.

'Aha! So you've decided to sew on that shoe button at last!' said the clockwork clown, coming up. 'Quite time, too – your shoe's fallen off heaps of times!'

'You be quiet,' said Amelia Jane.

'And while you're about it, why not mend that hole in your dress?' said a wooden skittle, hopping up. 'Or do you *like* holes in your dress, Amelia Jane?'

'You be quiet, too,' said Amelia, and jabbed at him with her needle. He hopped away with a chuckle.

He was soon back again. 'And what about your right stocking?' he said. 'It's got a great big hole in the heel. And what about . . . ?'

Amelia Jane jabbed at him again so hard that the thimble flew off her finger. It rolled away over the floor into a corner.

'Bother you, skittle!' said Amelia Jane, in a temper. 'Now you go and pick up that thimble and bring it back to me! Why do you tease me like this? I don't like you.'

'Shan't pick up your thimble!' said the skittle, enjoying himself. 'Silly old Amelia Jane!'

'Stop yelling at one another, and you go and pick up the thimble, skittle,' said the teddy bear, crossly. 'Can't you see I'm trying to read?'

The skittle didn't dare to disobey the big fat bear. He had once been rude to the bear and the bear had sat on him for a whole day, and the skittle hadn't liked that at all. The bear was so heavy.

So he picked up the thimble – but he didn't give it back

to Amelia Jane. No – he put it on his head for a hat! Then he walked up and down in a very silly way, saying, 'Look at my new hat! Oh, *do* look at my new hat!'

Everybody looked, of course, and all the toys laughed at the skittle because he really did look funny in a thimble-hat.

He took it off and bowed to them, and then put it back again.

'*Will* you give me my thimble?' cried Amelia Jane, in a rage. 'Give it to me AT ONCE!'

'Say "please", Amelia,' said the bear. 'You sound very rude.'

'I *shan't* say "please"!' cried Amelia. 'And don't you

interfere. Skittle, if you don't give me back my thimble at once I'll chase you and knock you over!'

'Can't catch *me*! Can't catch *me*!' said the skittle, who was really being very funny and very annoying. He ran here and there, and he kept taking his thimble-hat on and off to Amelia in a very ridiculous way.

Well, Amelia Jane wasn't going to let a skittle be cheeky to her, so up she got. She raced after the skittle, and he rushed away. But Amelia Jane caught him – and do you know what she did? Instead of taking the thimble off his head, she pushed it so hard that it went right over the poor skittle's nose, and he couldn't see a thing.

'Oh! Oh, it's so tight now I can't get it off!' yelled the skittle, trying to force the thimble off his head.

Amelia Jane laughed.

'That'll teach you to wear my thimble for a hat and be so rude to me,' she said.

'Help, help!' shouted the skittle. 'It's hurting me! Oooooooooh! Ow! OOOOOOOOOOH!'

'It really *is* hurting him,' said the bear, getting up. 'Dear, dear – I shall never finish my book today. Stand still, you silly skittle. I'll take the thimble off.'

Well, he tugged and he pulled, and he pulled and he tugged – but he couldn't get that thimble off!

Then Tom the toy soldier came up and had a try – but he couldn't get the thimble off either.

Amelia Jane tried – but it wasn't a bit of good; that thimble was jammed so hard on the skittle's head that it really could *not* be moved!

'You'll have to wear the thimble always,' said the bear at last.

The skittle lay down and yelled. 'I can't! I don't want to! Take it off, take it off! It's tight, I tell you!'

'We'll simply *have* to do something,' said Tom. 'Else the skittle will go on yelling for ever, and I don't think I could bear that.'

'Of *course* something must be done,' said the other skittles, who had popped up, looking very worried. 'Amelia Jane is very naughty.'

'That's nothing new,' said the bear. 'Dear me, do stop yelling, skittle. You'll wake up the household!'

Then the bear thought of something. 'Oh, I've got an idea,' he said. 'What about going out to ask the little pixie who lives in the pansy bed if he knows of a spell to help us. A Get-Loose Spell, perhaps.'

'A good idea,' said Tom. 'Amelia Jane, go and find the pixie and ask him.'

'What! In the middle of a dark night!' said Amelia Jane. 'No, thank you. And anyway, I don't like that pixie!'

'Amelia Jane, if you don't go and ask him, we shall take your best ribbon and hide it,' said the bear.

'Oh, no, don't do that!' said Amelia. 'It's my party ribbon. All right, you horrid things – I'll go. But I know a very good way of getting the thimble off the skittle.'

'How?' asked the toys.

'Chop off his head!' said Amelia Jane. 'He has so few brains that he'd never even notice his head was gone!'

'We *will* take away your best ribbon now,' said the

bear, as the skittle gave a loud yell of fright.

'No, no – I didn't mean it!' said Amelia Jane. 'I'll go this very minute to find the pixie.'

Well, off she went, climbing out of the window and down to the pansy bed.

The little pixie was there, wide awake.

'Pixie,' began Amelia, 'I want your help.'

'What will you give me for it?' asked the pixie, at once. He didn't like Amelia.

'Nothing,' said Amelia. 'Oh – let go of my foot, you horrid little pixie!'

'I'm taking your shoe for payment,' said the pixie. 'And the other one too. They will fit me nicely. Now, it's no good yelling. I've got them. I've no doubt you've been just as naughty as usual, so it serves you right. Now – what do you want my help for?'

Amelia Jane told him sulkily. 'The skittle is wearing my thimble jammed down hard on his head. How can we get it off?'

'Make the thimble bigger, of course,' said the pixie. 'Then his head will be too small for it and it will slip off.'

'But how can we make the thimble bigger?' asked Amelia Jane.

'Easy,' said the pixie. 'If you heat anything made of metal it becomes just a tiny bit larger – so heat the thimble, Amelia – and it will slip off the skittle's head.'

'But how can we heat it?' said Amelia, not really believing the pixie.

'Stand him on his head in hot water,' said the pixie. 'You could have thought of that yourself. Now go away. I want to try on your shoes.'

Amelia went back to the nursery. 'The pixie says that if we stand the skittle on his head in hot water, the thimble will get a bit larger and slip off,' said Amelia.

'I don't believe a word of it,' said the bear.

'Well, that's what he *said*,' said Amelia. 'He didn't tell me anything else. And I had to give him my shoes for that advice.'

'Hm,' said Tom. 'Well, poor old skittle – we'd better try it, anyway. Bear, put a little hot water into the basin,

will you? Don't put the plug in in case it gets too deep –
just let the water run in and out, and we'll pop the skittle
in on his head, and heat the thimble in the water.'

Well, the skittle howled and yelled and kicked up a great fuss, but the bear and the toy soldier were very firm with him. They turned him upside down and held him in the hot water, so that the heat warmed up the thimble on his head.

And will you believe it? – the thimble slipped off, just as the pixie had said it would. But alas – it rolled round the basin, and disappeared down the plughole! It was gone!

'Oh – my thimble, my thimble!' yelled Amelia Jane. But it was gone for good. Nobody ever saw it again.

'Serves you right, Amelia,' said the bear, turning the poor skittle the right way up again. 'Well, who would have thought the pixie knew a spell like that? Did *you* know that heat made things just a bit bigger, clockwork clown?'

'I never did,' said the clown.

But the funny thing is that it's *true*! So if ever a thimble gets stuck on one of your skittles you'll know what to do – stand him on his head in hot water and it will slip off!

And now Amelia Jane can't *bear* doing her mending, because she hasn't got a thimble and she pricks her finger all the time. Still, as the toys tell her – it's her own fault!

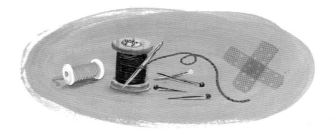

Amelia Jane Has a
Good Idea

Amelia Jane Has a Good Idea

The new teddy bear was very small indeed. The toys stared at him when he first came into the playroom, wondering what he was.

'Good gracious! I believe you're a teddy bear!' said Amelia Jane, the big, naughty doll. 'I thought you were a peculiar-shaped mouse.'

'Well, I'm not,' said the small bear, sharply, and pressed himself in the middle. 'Grrrrr! Hear me growl? Well, no mouse can growl. It can only squeak.'

'Yes. You're a bear all right,' said Tom, coming up. 'I hear you've come to live with us. Well, I'll show you your place in the toy-cupboard – right at the back there, look.'

'I don't like being at the back, it's too dark,' said the little bear. 'I'll be at the front here, by this big brick-box.'

'Oh, no you won't. That's *my* place when I want to sit in the toy-cupboard,' said Amelia Jane. 'And let me tell you this, small bear – if you live with us you'll have to take on lots of little bits of work. We all do. You'll have to wind up the clockwork clown when he runs down, you'll have to clean the dolls'-house windows, and you'll have to help the engine-driver polish his big red train.'

'Dear me, I don't think I want to do any of those things,' said the bear. 'I'm lazy. I don't like working.'

'Well, you'll just have to,' said Amelia Jane. 'Otherwise you won't get any of the biscuit crumbs that the children drop on the floor, you won't get any of the sweets in the toy sweet-shop – and we're allowed some every week – and you won't come to any parties. So there.'

'Pooh!' said the bear and stalked off to pick up some beads out of the bead-box and thread himself a necklace.

'He's vain as well as lazy,' said Tom in disgust. 'Hey, bear – what's your name? Or are you too lazy to have one?'

'My name is Sidney Gordon Eustace,' said the bear, haughtily. 'And please remember that I don't like being called Sid.'

'Sid!' yelled all the toys at once, and the bear looked furious. He turned his head away, and went on threading the beads.

'Sidney Gordon Eustace!' said the clown, with a laugh. 'I guess he gave himself those names. No sensible child would ever call a teddy bear that. Huh!'

The bear was not much use in the playroom. He

just would *not* do any of the jobs there at all. He went
surprisingly deaf when anyone called to him to come and
clean or polish or sweep. He would pretend to be asleep,
or just walk about humming a little tune as if nobody was
calling his name at all. It was most annoying.

'Sidney! Come and shake the mats for the dolls'-house dolls!' Tom called. No answer from Sidney at all.

'SIDNEY! Come here! You're not as deaf as all that!' The bear never even turned his head.

'Hey, Sidney Gordon Eustace – come and do your jobs!' yelled Tom. 'SID, SID, SID!'

No answer. 'All right!' shouted Tom, angrily. 'You shan't have that nice big crumb of chocolate biscuit we found under the table this morning.'

It was always the same whenever there was a job to be done. 'Sidney, come here!' But Sidney never came. He never did one single thing for any of the toys.

'What are we going to do about him?' said the big teddy bear. 'Amelia Jane – can't you think of a good idea?'

'Oh, yes,' said Amelia at once. 'I know what we'll do. We'll get Sidney-the-mouse to come and do the things that Sidney-the-bear should do – and he shall have all the crumbs and titbits that the bear should have. He won't like that – a little house-mouse getting all his treats!'

'Dear me – is the house-mouse's name Sidney, too?' said Tom in surprise. 'I never knew that before. When we want him we usually go to his hole and shout "Mouse" and he comes.'

'Well, I'll go and shout "Sidney",' said Amelia Jane, 'and you'll see – he'll come!' So she went to the little hole

at the bottom of the wall near the bookcase and shouted down it.

'Sidney! Sid-Sid-Sidney! We want you!'

The little bear, of course, didn't turn round – *he* wasn't going to come when his name was called. But someone very small came scampering up the passage to the hole-entrance. It was the tiny brown house-mouse, with bright black eyes and twitching whiskers.

'Ah, Sidney,' said Amelia Jane. 'Will you just come and shake the mats in the dolls' house, please? They are very dusty. We'll give you a big chocolate biscuit crumb and a drink of lemonade out of the little teapot if you will.'

'Can I drink out of the spout?' said the tiny mouse, pleased. 'I like drinking out of the spout.'

'Yes, of course,' said Amelia Jane.

The little mouse set about shaking the mats vigorously, and the job was soon done.

'Isn't Sidney wonderful?' said Amelia in a loud voice to the others. 'Sidney-the-mouse, I mean, of course, not silly Sidney-the-bear. He wouldn't have the strength to shake mats like that, poor thing. Sidney, here's the chocolate biscuit crumb and there's the teapot full of lemonade.'

Sidney the bear didn't like this at all. Fancy making a fuss of a silly little mouse, and giving him treats like that. He would very much have liked the crumb and the lemonade himself. He pressed himself in the middle and growled furiously when the mouse had gone.

'Don't have that mouse here again,' he said. 'I don't

like hearing somebody else being called Sidney. Anyway, I don't believe his name *is* Sidney. It's not a name for a mouse.'

'Well, for all you know, his name might be Sidney Gordon Eustace just like yours,' said Amelia Jane at once.

'Pooh! Whoever heard of a mouse having a grand name like that?' said the bear.

'Well, next time you won't do a job, we'll call all three names down the hole,' said Amelia, 'and see if the little mouse will answer to them!'

Next night there was going to be a party. Everyone had to help to get ready for it. Amelia Jane called to the little bear.

'Sidney! Come and set the tables for the party. Sidney, do you hear me?'

Sidney did, but he pretended not to, of course. Set party tables! Not he! So he went deaf again, and didn't even turn his head.

'Sidney Gordon Eustace, do as you're told or you won't come to the party,' bawled the big teddy bear in a fine old rage.

The little bear didn't answer. Amelia Jane gave a sudden grin.

'Never mind,' she said. 'We'll get Sidney Gordon Eustace, the little mouse, to come and set the tables. He does them beautifully and never breaks a thing. He can come to the party afterwards then. I'll call him.'

The little bear turned his head. 'He won't answer to *that* name, you know he won't!' he said, scornfully. 'Call away! No mouse ever had a name as grand as mine.'

Amelia Jane went to the mouse-hole and called down it.

'Sidney Gordon Eustace, are you there?' she called. 'If you are at home, come up and help us. Sidney Gordon Eustace, are you there?'

And at once there came the pattering of tiny feet, and with a loud squeak the little mouse peeped out of his hole, his whiskers quivering.

'Ah – you are at home,' said Amelia. 'Well, dear little Sidney, will you set the tables for us? We're going to have a party.'

The mouse was delighted. He was soon at work, and in a short while the four tables were set with tiny table-cloths and china. Then he went to help the dolls'-house dolls to cut sandwiches. The bear watched all this out of the corner of his eye. He was quite amazed that the mouse had come when he was called Sidney Gordon Eustace – goodness, fancy a little mouse owning a name like that!

He was very cross when he saw that the mouse was going to the party. Amelia Jane found him a red ribbon to tie round his neck and one for his long tail. He was given a place at the biggest table, and everyone made a fuss of him.

'Good little Sidney! You do work well! Whatever should we do without you? What will you have to eat?'

The mouse ate a lot. *Much* too much, the little bear thought. He didn't go to the party. He hadn't been asked and he didn't quite like to go because there was no chair for him and no plate. But, oh, all those nice things to eat! *Why* hadn't he been sensible and gone to set the tables?

'Goodnight, Sidney Gordon Eustace,' said Amelia to the delighted mouse. 'We've loved having you.'

Now, after this kind of thing had happened three or four times the bear got tired of it.

He hated hearing people yell for 'Sidney, Sidney!' down the mouse-hole, or to hear the mouse addressed as Sidney Gordon Eustace. It was really too bad. Also, the mouse was getting all the titbits and the treats. The bear didn't like that either.

So the next time that there was a job to be done the bear decided to do it. He suddenly heard Tom say 'Hallo! The big red engine is very smeary. It wants a polish again. I'll go and call Sidney.'

Tom went to the mouse-hole and began to call down it. 'Sidney, Sidney, Sidney!'

But before the mouse could answer, Sidney the bear rushed up to Tom. 'Yes! Did you call me? What do you want me to do?'

'Dear me – you're not as deaf as usual!' said Tom, surprised. 'Well, go and polish the red engine, then. You can have a sweet out of the toy sweet shop if you do it properly.'

Sidney did do it properly. Tom came and looked at the engine and so did Amelia Jane. 'Very nice,' said Amelia. 'Give him a big sweet, Tom.'

The bear was pleased. Aha! He had done the mouse out of a job. The toys had been pleased with him, and the sweet was delicious.

And after that, dear me, you should have seen Sidney the bear rush up whenever his name was called. 'Yes, yes – here I am. What do you want me to do?'

Very soon the little mouse was not called up from the hole any more, and Sidney the bear worked hard and was friendly and sensible. The toys began to like him, and Sidney liked them too.

But one thing puzzled Tom and the big teddy bear, and they asked Amelia Jane about it.

'Amelia Jane – HOW did you know that the mouse's name was Sidney Gordon Eustace?'

'It isn't,' said Amelia with a grin.

'But it must be,' said Tom. 'He always came when you called him by it.'

'I know – but he'd come if you called *any* name down his hole,' said Amelia. 'Go and call what name you like – he'll come! It's the calling he answers, not the name! He doesn't even know what names are!'

'Good gracious!' said Tom and the bear, and they went to the mouse-hole.

'William!' called Tom, and up came the mouse. He was given a crumb and went down again.

'Polly-Wolly-Doodle!' shouted the big bear, and up came the mouse for another crumb.

'Boot-polish!' shouted Tom, and up came the mouse.

'Tomato soup!' cried the big bear. And it didn't matter what name was yelled down the hole, the mouse always came up. He came because he heard a loud shout, that was all. Amelia Jane went off into fits of laughter when the mouse came up at different calls. 'Penny stamp! Cough-

drop! Sid-Sid-Sid! Dickory-Dock! Rub-a-dub-dub!'

The mouse's nose appeared at the hole each time. How the toys laughed – all except Sidney the bear!

He didn't laugh. He felt very silly indeed. Oh, dear – what a trick Amelia Jane had played on him! But suddenly he began to laugh, too. 'It's funny,' he cried. 'It's funny!'

It certainly was. Amelia *would* think of a good idea like that, wouldn't she?

Amelia Jane Goes Up the Tree

Amelia Jane Goes Up The Tree

It was springtime, and the birds were all nesting. Amelia Jane was most excited.

'The birds are building their nests,' she said. 'They are laying eggs.'

'Well, they do that every year,' said Tom.

'I want to make a collection of birds' eggs,' said Amelia Jane, grandly.

'You naughty doll!' said the clockwork clown. 'You know quite well you mustn't take birds' eggs.'

'Well, I don't see why birds can't spare me one or two of their eggs,' said Amelia. 'After all – they can't count.'

'Amelia Jane, you know quite well that birds get dreadfully upset if they see anyone near their nests,' said the teddy bear. 'You know that sometimes they get very frightened, and they desert their nests – leave them altogether – so that the eggs get cold, and never hatch out.'

'Oh, don't lecture me so!' said Amelia Jane. 'I said I wanted to make a collection of birds' eggs, and so I am going to. You can't stop me.'

'You are a very bad doll,' said the clown, and he turned his back on Amelia. 'I don't like you one bit.'

Amelia Jane laughed. She was feeling in a very naughty mood. She looked out of the window, down into a big chestnut tree. In the fork of a branch was a nest. It belonged to a thrush.

'There's a thrush's nest just down there,' said Amelia. 'I wish I could climb down. But I can't. It's too dangerous. Perhaps I could climb up.'

'How could you do that?' said the curly-haired doll, in a scornful voice. 'Don't be silly. None of us could climb up that tall trunk!'

But the next day Amelia Jane was excited. 'The gardener has put a ladder up the chestnut tree!' she said. 'He has, really. He is cutting off some of the bigger branches, because they knock against the low roof of the shed.

I shall slip down, wait till the gardener has gone to his dinner, and then climb the ladder!'

'Amelia Jane! You don't mean to say you really *are* going to rob a bird's nest!' cried the clown.

'Oh yes,' said Amelia. 'Why should the bird mind if one or two eggs are taken? She will probably be glad that she hasn't so many hungry beaks to fill, when the eggs hatch out!'

So, to the horror of the watching toys, Amelia Jane slipped downstairs, out of the garden door and up to the ladder, as soon as the gardener had gone to his dinner.

The toys all pressed their noses to the window and watched her.

'She's climbing the ladder!' said the clown. 'She really is!'

'She's up to the top of it!' squeaked the clockwork mouse.

'She's going right into the tree!' cried the teddy bear, and he almost broke the window with his nose, he pressed so hard against it.

Amelia Jane was climbing the tree very well. She was a big strong doll, and she swung herself up easily. She soon came to the big thrush's nest. The mother-thrush was not there.

I suppose she has gone to stretch her wings a little, thought Amelia Jane. She stretched out her hand and put it into the nest. There were four eggs there, and they felt smooth and warm. Amelia Jane took one and put it into the pocket of her red dress. Then she took another, and

put that in her second pocket.

'There!' she said. 'Two will be enough, I think. I can start a very nice collection with two. How pretty they are! I like them.'

She sat up in the tree for a little while, enjoying the sound of the wind in the leaves and liking the swaying of the bough she sat on. It was so exciting.

'I'd better go back now,' she said. 'I don't want to be here when the mother-thrush comes back.'

So she began to climb down the tree again. But, after a while, she heard a noise. It was someone whistling. She peeped down between the leaves.

'It's the gardener!' said Amelia Jane in dismay. 'Oh dear, I hope he isn't coming up the tree now.'

He wasn't. He was doing something else – something that filled Amelia Jane with great dismay.

'He's taking away the ladder! Oh my! It's gone! However am I to get down again? The ladder's gone!'

It certainly *was* gone. The gardener, still whistling, carried it away for another job. And there was Amelia Jane, left high up the tree!

She sat there for a long time. She heard the thrush come back again to her nest. She heard the wind in the trees. She saw the toys in the nursery looking out at her in surprise, wondering why she didn't climb down and come back.

'I do feel lonely and frightened,' said Amelia to herself, when the day went and the cold night began to come. 'I shall be very afraid up here in the dark. Oh dear, why ever did I think of climbing the tree and stealing eggs? It's a punishment for me, it really is!'

She began to cry. And when Amelia Jane cried she made a noise. She sobbed and gulped and howled. It was a dreadful noise.

A small pixie, who lived in the primrose bed below, heard the noise and wondered what it was. So she flew up into the tree to see.

'Oh, it's you, Amelia Jane,' said the pixie. 'What's the matter? You're keeping me awake with that dreadful noise.'

'I can't get down,' sobbed Amelia. 'I want to get back to the nursery, and I can't.'

'Whatever made you climb up?' asked the pixie. But Amelia was too ashamed to tell her.

'Please help me,' begged the big doll. 'I am so unhappy.'

'Well, maybe the thrush who lives higher up the tree can help you,' said the pixie, and she flew up to see. Amelia Jane felt most uncomfortable. She had taken eggs from the thrush's nest. Oh dear! How she wished she hadn't!

The pixie flew back again, and the big brown thrush was with her.

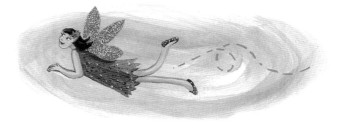

'Here's the thrush,' said the pixie. 'She is very sad and unhappy tonight, because some horrid person stole two of her precious eggs, but she is very kind, and although she is sad she will help you.'

'Yes, I will help you, help you, help you,' sang the
thrush sweetly. 'I am sad, sad, sad, but I will help you,
big, big doll.'

'How can you help me?' asked Amelia in surprise.

'I can guide you right up the tree,' said the thrush. 'I know the way. I can bring you right up to the nursery window-sill, and you can knock on the window and get the toys to let you in. Then you will be safe, safe, safe!'

'Oh, you *are* kind!' said Amelia Jane. She turned to follow the thrush up the tree.

'Hold on to one of my tail-feathers,' said the thrush kindly. 'Don't be afraid of pulling it out.'

Amelia held on to a feather, and the thrush guided her gently up the dark tree. After a little while she stopped and spoke.

'Big doll, can you see my nest just here? It is such a nice, comfortable one. It is very dark now, but perhaps you can just see two eggs gleaming in the cup. Aren't they lovely?'

Amelia Jane could see them gleaming in the half-darkness. The thrush went on, half speaking, half singing.

'You know, I had more eggs than those you see. But whilst I was away this morning someone took two, took two, took two. It nearly broke my heart. Now I shall only have two children instead of four. Can you imagine anyone bad enough to steal from a little bird like me?'

Amelia Jane felt the two eggs in her pockets, and she began to sob. 'What's the matter?' asked the kindly thrush; and she pressed her warm, feathery body close to Amelia to comfort her.

'Oh, brown thrush, oh, brown thrush,' sobbed Amelia. 'I took your eggs. I've got them in my pockets. Let me put them back into your nest, please, please! They are still lovely and warm, and I haven't broken them. I'm the horrid person that took them, but I'm dreadfully sorry now!'

She took the warm eggs from her pockets and put them gently into the nest.

'Now push me down the tree; do anything you like to punish me!' said Amelia Jane. 'I know I deserve it.'

'What a foolish doll you are!' said the thrush, very happy

to see her eggs once more. 'Because you were unkind to me is no reason why I should now be unkind to you. I am happy again, so I want to make you happy, too! Come along, hold on to my tail-feather, and we'll go higher till we come to the window-sill!'

So up they went, with Amelia wiping her eyes on her skirt every now and again because she was so ashamed of herself and so grateful to the thrush for forgiving her and being kind to her.

They came to the window-sill, and Amelia rapped on it. The teddy bear, who was just the other side, called the clown, and together they opened the window. Amelia slipped inside. She said goodbye to the thrush, and then looked at the toys.

'Whatever happened to you?' said the clown. 'Did you take the eggs? Surely that was the thrush helping you just now!'

'I did take the eggs, but I've given them back, and I'm ashamed of myself for taking them,' said Amelia in a very small voice. 'I shall never, never do such a thing again in my life. I'm going to be a Good Doll now.'

'Hmmm,' said the clown. 'We've heard that before, Amelia Jane! We'll see what the thrush has to say tomorrow!'

I heard her singing the next day, and do you know what she sang? She sang: 'Took two, took two, put them back, put them back, put them back, sweet, sweet, sweet!' Listen, and maybe you'll hear her singing that, too!

Goodbye, Amelia Jane!

Goodbye, Amelia Jane!

The toys played a trick on Amelia Jane the other day.

Amelia Jane was always playing tricks on all the toys in the nursery. There was no end to her mischief. If she didn't think of one thing, she thought of another.

There was the time when she collected worms in the garden and popped them all into Tom's shut umbrella. They wriggled about there and couldn't get out, poor things.

And then Amelia sent Tom out into the garden to fetch her hanky from the garden seat. It was raining, of course, so she gave him his umbrella.

'Better put this up,' she said, and he did. And out slithered all the worms, on top of his head and down his neck, as soon as he got out into the garden in the rain.

The worms fled into holes very thankfully, but Tom got such a fright that he ran straight into the pond and got wet through.

He was very, very angry with Amelia Jane, but she only laughed.

'You shouldn't let worms nest in your umbrella,' she said.

Another time, Amelia took the teapot out of the toy tea-set and filled it with hot water from the tap. Then she climbed up to the roof of the dolls' house and poured the hot water down the chimney.

The little dolls'-house dolls rushed out of the front door in fright, with water trickling down the stairs after them, and Amelia Jane nearly fell off the roof with laughing.

She was well scolded for that bit of mischief, but she

wouldn't even say she was sorry.

The toys had a meeting about her.

'I'm tired of Amelia Jane,' said the toy soldier.

'So am I,' said the clockwork clown. 'She took my key away yesterday for about the fiftieth time.'

'Can't we get rid of her?' said the teddy bear.

'We've often tried,' said the clockwork mouse. 'But we never have.'

'I've got an idea,' said Tom, his eyes shining brightly. 'It's a small idea at the moment – but if we talk about it, it might grow into a big one and be really good.'

'What is it?' asked the clockwork clown.

'Well – you know you can slide down the stairs on a tray, don't you?' said Tom.

Everyone nodded.

'That's my idea,' said Tom. 'It's only just that. I haven't thought any more than that.'

'It seems rather silly,' said the bear. 'Did you mean to get Amelia Jane to slide down the stairs on a tray, or what?'

'I don't know,' said Tom. 'I tell you, I hadn't thought

any further than I said.'

'Ooooh!' said the clown. '*Could* we make her slide down on a tray – push her very, very hard . . . ?'

'And have the front door open so that she shot right out in a hurry,' went on the bear.

'And have the garden gate open so that she'd shoot out there, too,' said the clown.

'And then down the hill she'd go, whizz-bang, faster and faster and faster,' said the clockwork mouse, excitedly.

'And splash into the stream on her tray, and off it would go like a boat, all the way down to the sea!' finished Tom, his face beaming with excitement.

'And we'd never, never see her again, the bad, naughty doll,' said the bear.

'No, we wouldn't. We'd shout, "Goodbye, Amelia Jane!" when she flew out of the front door, and that would be that,' said Tom. 'See what my little idea has grown to – a great big one. I thought it would!'

Well, the toys talked and talked about their idea, and got very excited about it indeed. Surely they could at last get rid of that naughty Amelia Jane!

Amelia didn't know anything about all this, of course. She was out in the garden collecting a few more worms to play another trick. Tom had time to get out the big tin tray from its corner and rub soap underneath it to make it more slippery.

'We'll play our trick when everyone is out tomorrow,' he decided. 'If I stand on a chair in the hall I can open the front door all right. Now, don't say a word about our plan, any of you!'

The next afternoon the house was very quiet because everyone had gone out. Tom took the tin tray and banged hard on it. 'Boom, diddy-boom!'

'Stop that noise,' said Amelia Jane, crossly. 'I want to have a snooze.'

'All right. Have one,' said Tom. 'We are all going to the top of the stairs to play at sliding down on this tea-tray. We'll have a lovely time – and we don't want *you*, Amelia Jane!'

Well, that was quite enough to make Amelia want to come, of course! 'I'm coming, too,' she said. 'And I guess I'll go faster down the stairs than any of you!'

Off they all went to the top of the stairs. Tom ran down, got a chair, stood on it, and opened the front door. He ran back and had his turn at sliding down. The tray went down to the bottom, bumpity-bumpity-bump, slid a little way down the hall and stopped. Aha! If they all pushed hard when Amelia Jane had her turn, it would most certainly fly out of the door, down the path, out of the gate and away down the hill to the stream at the bottom!

'I want my turn, I want mine!' shouted Amelia, and she got on to the tray. She held tight – and the toy soldier, the bear, the clockwork clown, the mouse and another doll all pushed as hard as ever they could.

Whooooooosh! You should have seen that tray fly down the stairs at top speed! Amelia's breath was quite taken

away. Her hair and her dress flew out behind her, and she stared in fright. This was a much faster journey than she had imagined!

Down to the bottom of the stairs – along the hall at top

speed – out of the open door – down the slippery front path – out of the open gate – and whoooooosh – down the steep hill that led to the stream!

'Goodbye, Amelia Jane!' shouted the toys. 'Goodbye, goodbye!'

'She's gone,' said the bear, after a pause. 'Really gone. She'll never tease us again.'

'Never,' said Tom, pleased. 'She's played her last trick on us.'

'She deserved to be shot off like that,' said the clown. 'Now let's play at sliding trays downstairs all by ourselves.'

They played for quite a long time. Then they went back to the nursery to have a drink of water.

'I just hope Amelia Jane didn't tip off the tray going

down the hill, and hurt herself,' said the bear, suddenly.
'And I just hope she didn't fall into the stream and get

drowned,' said the clown.

'It seems a bit funny without her,' said the mouse. 'Er – you don't suppose we were dreadfully unkind, do you?'

'Not a bit,' said Tom. 'She deserved to be sent off like that.'

'But you wouldn't want her to hurt herself, would you?' said the bear, solemnly. 'You know – I keep on and on thinking what would happen if she tipped off the tray going down-hill – suppose she fell under a bus – or . . .'

The clockwork mouse gave a squeal of fright. 'Don't say things like that. They frighten me. You make me feel as if I want Amelia Jane back.'

'Perhaps she wasn't as bad as she seemed,' said the bear. 'You know – I don't feel very nice about playing that trick on her now. I feel sort of uncomfortable.'

'Pooh!' said Tom, but he didn't say any more.

Well, what *had* happened to Amelia Jane? She had slid out into the front garden and out of the gate, and down the hill at top speed. She was very frightened indeed. Why had the toys shouted goodbye? Was it a trick they

had played on her to get rid of her? Amelia Jane wailed aloud as she shot down the hill. Oh dear, oh dear, had she been so dreadful that the toys wanted to get rid of her like that?

'I'm going straight into the stream!' she squealed, and splash, into the water she went. She clung to the tray. It didn't sink, but bobbed on the surface, with a very wet Amelia Jane clinging on top. Down the stream she went, bobbing on the waves.

She floated for a very long way. Then the tray bumped into the bank, stuck into some weeds and stopped. Amelia thankfully crawled off on to the land. She was wet and cold and tired. She could see a dog not far off and she was frightened of him.

Where could she hide? What was that lying on the grass over there? A bicycle! It had a basket behind the saddle, and Amelia Jane staggered off to it. She squeezed into the basket, and stuffed an old bit of newspaper over herself. Now, perhaps, nobody, not even the dog, would see her.

She fell asleep and dreamed of the toys. She dreamt that they were all cross with her, and she cried in her sleep.

'Don't be cross with me. I'll be good, I'll be good.'

Then she woke up – and dear me, she was wobbling from side to side in the basket. Somebody had picked up the bicycle, mounted it, and was now riding away down the river path – with Amelia Jane tucked into the basket at the back.

Oh, dear! thought Amelia, in a panic. 'Now where am I going? I'm miles and miles away from home – and from all the toys. I wish I was back again. Wouldn't I be good if I could only get back to the nursery! But the toys wouldn't be pleased to see me at all. They'd turn me out again.'

On she went and on. Miles and miles it seemed to Amelia Jane, and she grew cramped and cold in the basket. And then, at last, the rider stopped and jumped off.

He flung his bicycle against something, and walked off, whistling.

Amelia Jane peeped out. The bicycle was against a wall near a back door. She crawled out of the basket, and almost fell to the ground. She ran to the door. If only she could get into a house, she could hide.

In she went, and somebody jumped in surprise as the big doll ran past. Amelia tore into the hall and up the stairs. She almost fell inside a room, and stopped there, panting in fright.

And will you believe it, she was back in the nursery again – and there were all the toys she knew, staring at her in amazement – the toy soldier, the bear, the clown, the mouse and everyone!

She had come all the way home in the basket of the bicycle belonging to one of the children! He had gone to

the river that day, and then had cycled all the way back – and Amelia Jane was in his basket. What a very, very peculiar thing!

'You said goodbye to me – but here I am again,' said Amelia, in a funny, shaky sort of voice. 'It seems as if you c-c-c-can't get rid of me!'

She burst into tears – and then everyone ran to comfort her. She was patted and fussed, and even Tom kept saying he was glad to see her back.

'Oh, dear – this is all so nice,' said Amelia at last. 'I won't be mischievous again, toys. I won't play tricks any more. I'll be just as good as gold!'

'We don't believe you,' said Tom. 'But never mind – we're glad to have you back, you bad, naughty doll. We never *really* want to say goodbye to you, Amelia Jane!'

I don't either. What about you?

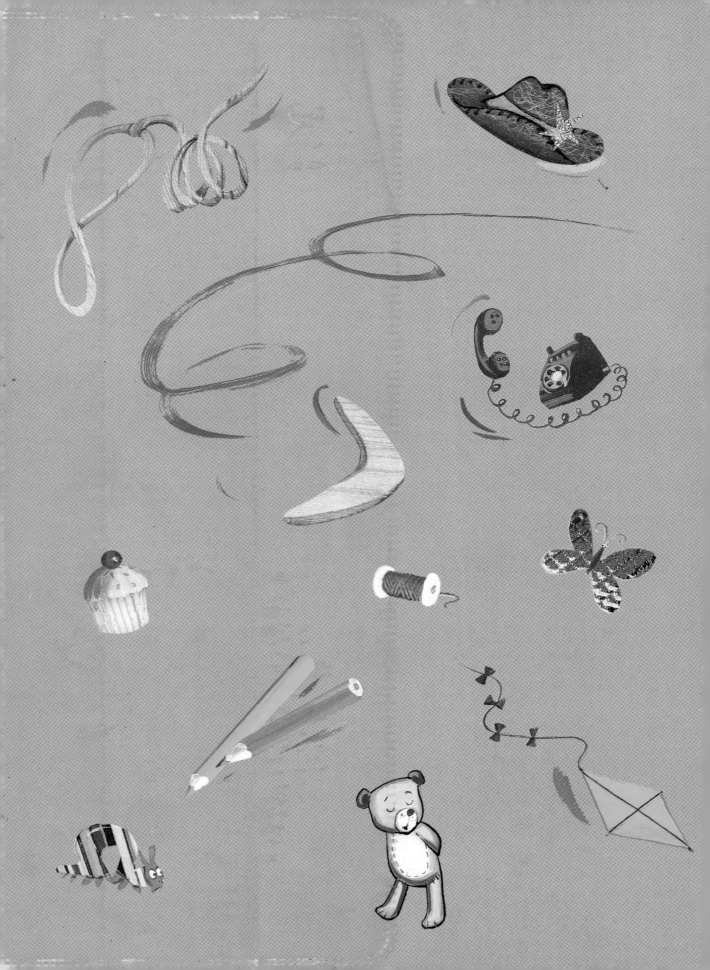